The Newest
MIND-BLOWING
Management Insights
from the Last Century

A Comprehensive Analysis

Ali Parnian

DEDICATION

I dedicate this book to my family, who supported me while I travelled the world to meet with thought leaders and conduct extensive research to accomplish this feat.

I also dedicate this book to all of the future readers who will purchase multiple copies of this book for all of their colleagues, friends, family and acquaintances. I sincerely appreciate all of you who strive to share the gift of knowledge while helping me pay for unnecessary luxury goods that will likely not incrementally improve my happiness and yet I am okay with that.

CONTENTS

ACKNOWLEDGMENTS

I would like to thank the extensive team that helped put this together, you know who you are!

CHAPTER 1
TOP NEW MANAGEMENT INSIGHTS 1920 - 1980:

The mind blowing new management insights below were highly regarded and utilized at different times within many organizations between 1920 to 1980. For more detail on the concepts in bold below, use Google to search by going to https://www.google.com from your smartphone or computer browser. You will be sure to find millions of lengthy articles that espouse the virtues of the content below.

WARNING: The concepts you are about to read are simple yet powerful. It is highly recommend you read this section just one bullet at a time and preferably in a seated position in case you start to feel unbalanced or overwhelmed by the sheer impact these concepts may have on your senses.

1. Establish a **company vision** so you know where you want to go.
2. Formulate a **strategy** so you know how you will get there.
3. **Hire good people** because good people are good.
4. **Fire bad people quickly** because they suck and the longer they stay the more the good people will start sucking or leave.
5. **Communicate often** because people forget.
6. **Communicate often** because people forget.
7. Give people **measurable and specific goals** so expectations are clear.
8. **Managers should check-in** with their team often because as a manager they should actually be managing.
9. **Focus on the most important things** first to accomplish goals.
10. **Develop your employees** to make them be better.
11. **Culture is important.**

CHAPTER 2
TOP NEW MANAGEMENT INSIGHTS 1981-2000

Our research showed that there was nothing new in this 20 year period, just the same old concepts recycled and rebranded.

CHAPTER 3
TOP NEW MANAGEMENT Insights 2001-2010

Still nothing.

CHAPTER 4
TOP NEW MANAGEMENT INSIGHTS 2011-2019

None. Nada. Zip. Zero. Still nothing!

CHAPTER 5
SYNTHESIS

Our research shows that there have been no mind-blowing insights in management for several decades. People don't change much and the challenges and solutions to managing the human condition are fundamentally the same. If you feel differently, I would love to hear from you. Please share any management breakthroughs that I may have missed by visiting AliParnian.com.

CHAPTER 6
DECISION

All of the webinars, seminars, workshops, retreats and training you may have consumed over the years were likely just repackaged versions of the principles we covered in depth in Chapter 1.

The good news is that you now know everything there is to know about the most impactful business management principles ever created and you have a decision to make.

You can either continue to pay for consultants, coaches, teachers, gurus, workshops, boot camps, seminars or courses in hopes of learning new concepts, or, you can spend your time and money doing things that you actually value and enjoy.

We have provided you with blank pages in Chapter 7 as a safe place where you can list all of the things you would like to do with the time and money saved by not paying to re-learn management insights covered in this book.

CHAPTER 7
THE FUTURE AWAITS

Use the following blank pages to plan your future and how you will spend all of the time and money saved by reading this book.

Please remember, this is a safe space, there are no right or wrong answers. Let your imagination go wild! There are no ideas too big or too small to jot down. You can even doodle pictures or glue magazine clippings to use the pages as an inspiration board to map out your life. Your future awaits!

CHAPTER 8
WHAT ABOUT BUSINESS RESULTS?

After reflecting on the management insights explained in Chapter 1 and listing all of the things that you wish to do with the time and money saved in Chapter 7, you may be asking yourself, "What about business results?"

Well, your tenacity and dedication have paid off. Thank you for sticking with it. You have made it to the final chapter.

Since the management insights have not changed in decades, the logical next step is to actually apply those tried and true proven insights to your organization.

This may sound simple, but it's not. Knowing what should be done and actually doing it effectively are two different things entirely.

I know that eating a nutritious low calorie diet and exercising will make me feel better and live a longer life, and yet I don't do this consistently.

Management insights are even harder to implement because they need to be applied consistently to an entire organization to be effective…and doing so won't even extend people's lives!

So before looking for the next management magic bullet, seek instead to find an organization that specializes in implementing proven management practices in simple and effective ways so they can be scaled and sustained throughout your organization. For recommendations go to AliParnian.com.

ABOUT THE AUTHOR

Ali Parnian is a business writer, leadership coach and management consultant who works with diverse leadership teams and organizations around the world to help drive tangible results.

52318068R00084

Made in the USA
San Bernardino, CA
07 September 2019